Waiting for Goldie

SUSAN GATES

Illustrated by Jane Cope

Oxford University Press 1996

Oxford University Press, Walton Street, Oxford OX2 6DP

Oxford New York
Athens Auckland Bangkok Bogota Bombay
Buenos Aires Calcutta Cape Town Dar es Salaam
Delhi Florence Hong Kong Istanbul Karachi
Kuala Lumpur Madras Madrid Melbourne
Mexico City Nairobi Paris Singapore
Taipei Tokyo Toronto

and associated companies in
Berlin Ibadan

Oxford is a trade mark of Oxford University Press

Printed in Great Britain by Ebenezer Baylis

Illustrations by Jane Cope

Photograph of Susan Gates © Pauline Holbrook

1

Where is she?

I've got an important job to do. I'm really nervous about it. It's a big responsibility. I'm in Grandad's garden, sitting outside his pigeon loft. I'm waiting for Goldie to come home.

Goldie's proper name is Goldeneye. She's Grandad's champion racing pigeon.

She's famous. She's won loads of cups. This morning she was released two hundred miles away with lots of other pigeons. And now she's racing back home.

'Come on, Goldie. Come on, Goldie. Come on, Goldie!'

That's me, calling Goldeneye back home. But I can't see her yet. She should be flying in any minute.

I really want Goldie to win this race. I want to give Grandad some good news when I see him tonight in hospital.

'Fly outside. Go on, get going!' I'm letting the other pigeons out to welcome Goldie home. They swoop round and round the loft. Then they settle on the roof. My eyes search the blue sky. Still no sign of Goldie.

'That's her!'

But it isn't. It's just a wild pigeon. Not Grandad's champion racer.

'Calm down, Danny!' I tell myself. That's what Grandad would have said: 'Calm down, Danny. Calm down, son!'

But it's hard to be calm. This job is very important. I'll tell you why.

Before a race they put a rubber ring on every pigeon's leg. When Goldie comes back I've got to catch her, as soon as she lands. I've got to take her ring off, as fast as I can, and put it in a little metal tube. I've got to put that tube in Grandad's special timing clock. That records the time that Goldie finished the race.

But I'll have to move like lightning. I can't waste a second. I've got to get that ring into that clock as quickly as I can!

So that's why I'm nervous, waiting for Goldie. I'm getting more nervous every minute. Because Goldie should be here by now.

'Come on, Goldie, come on, Goldie.'

But the sky is blue and empty.

Maybe she isn't coming back.

'No!' I tell myself. 'Goldie always comes back.'

Thump, thump, thump. What's that? It's my heart pounding. That's how nervous I am.

'Calm down, son,' I tell myself.

But where is she? She's never been this late before. What am I going to tell Grandad?

Grandad says you can tell a lot by looking in a pigeon's eyes. You can tell if they're going to be a good racer. Goldie has got golden eyes. That's very rare. Grandad says he's never had a pigeon like her. She's one in a million, he says.

But she isn't coming home. Wait, there's a flutter in the sky!

I look up. 'Is that you, Goldie?' But it's only a crow.

I'm giving up hope. But I wait until it's nearly dark. Then I lock the other pigeons in the loft and padlock the door.

I've got to see Grandad tonight at the hospital. What am I going to tell him?

2

Grandad

I haven't told Mum and Dad yet about
Goldie being missing. They wouldn't
understand. They're not interested in
Grandad's pigeons.

I tried to get out of coming to see
Grandad. I told Mum, 'I can't go to
the hospital. I don't feel very well!'

But she said, 'Come on, Danny.
He'll be expecting you. He'll be really
disappointed if you don't come to see
him.'

So now we're walking into Grandad's ward. There are flowers everywhere but it doesn't smell of flowers. It smells of disinfectant. And everyone's talking in whispers, as if they're in a church.

Where's Grandad? I've just walked right past him! He's in a high white bed. And he doesn't look like my Grandad because he's had a shave and he hasn't got his scruffy old jumper on. He's got smart white and blue pyjamas on.

'Say hello to your Grandad, Danny,' says Mum, pushing me towards the bed.

But the words won't come out of my mouth.

There's a machine by Grandad's bed.
It looks a bit like a TV with green
wavy lines on the screen.

Grandad's joined to the machine by
wires stuck to his chest. I know what's
wrong with him. No one told me but I
heard Mum and Dad talking about it.

'He's had a heart attack,' Mum told
Dad. 'Only a very mild one. But it's a
warning. He'll have to take it easy
from now on.'

Mum puts some grapes on
Grandad's bed. 'What did the doctor
say?' she asks him.

'I don't want grapes,' says Grandad. 'I want my pigeon racing magazines.'

He looks a bit feeble. But he still sounds like the same old Grandad! He's as grumpy as ever. He's like that with lots of people. But never with his pigeons. Or with me.

'Now Danny,' Grandad says to me. 'Don't keep me waiting! Did Goldie win? Did my champion racer win?'

I knew he'd ask me that question. I bet he's been thinking about it all day. What am I going to tell him? My mind's all confused. It's going round, *whirr, whirr*, like a washing machine on fast spin.

Grandad sits up in bed. There are two red spots burning on his cheeks. 'Has the cat got your tongue, Danny?' asks Grandad. 'There's nothing wrong with Goldie, is there?'

Of course there is. Goldie's missing. She might even be dead. But how can I tell him that?

'Those peregrine falcons didn't get her, did they?' shouts Grandad. 'Those ones that are nesting in the old quarry? They're a menace, those hawks! Someone should get rid of them! Someone should pull down that nest. Then they'll go somewhere else!'

Beep, beep, beep, beep, beep!
Grandad's machine is going berserk.

The green wavy lines are going up and
down, up and down like a stormy sea.

'Now, now, now, now, now!' says
Mum, clicking her tongue. 'Don't get
yourself upset!'

She looks angrily at me. 'Why don't
you say something, Danny? You can
see Grandad is upset! Goldie is all
right, isn't she? Of course the falcons
didn't get her! Tell him Goldie is all
right!'

I know I'm going to do it before I
open my mouth. I'm going to tell
Grandad a lie.

Well, what else can I do? If I tell him the truth he might get very poorly. He might even have another heart attack. And then it'll be all my fault.

'Goldie got home at three o'clock,' I tell Grandad.

My stomach's all scrunched up. I feel really scared. Because, usually, Grandad can tell when I'm lying. He looks into my eyes, just like he looks into his pigeons' eyes. And he says, 'You're lying to me, Danny. I can tell from your eyes.'

But this time he doesn't say it. He believes the lie.

'Nice timing!' he says. 'I bet she won that race.'

'Yes,' I tell him. 'She probably did.'

'I knew it,' says Grandad, settling back on his pillows. 'I always knew she was a winner! You've really made me feel better, Danny! I want to get better and get out of this place and see my Goldie. You've given me something to look forward to!'

3

The falcon's nest

I'm still hoping Goldie might come
back. But it's the day after the race and
there's no sign of her. I'm sitting
outside Grandad's pigeon loft staring
into the sky. I daren't even blink in
case I miss her.

'Come on, Goldie, come on, Goldie,
come on, Goldie.'

Sometimes racing pigeons turn up days after a race. They get lost, or hit bad weather. But that's never happened to Goldie. She always comes home, right on time.

'Come on, Goldie.'

I've known Goldie ever since she was an egg. I've known her since she was a floppy pink chick. I helped Grandad look after her. I've held her in my hands after a race and felt her little heart beating, *pat-a-pat-a-pat*.

She's beautiful. She's pale grey. She's got shiny green and blue feathers on her neck that sparkle like sequins.

'Come on, Goldie.' I can't stop saying that. I've been whispering it ever since I woke up, like a magic spell. 'Come on, Goldie, come on, Goldie.' But it can't be a very good spell. It's not working. It's not bringing Goldie back home.

What am I going to do? I want my Grandad to get better. I want him to come out of hospital. But when he comes out he'll come straight to his pigeon loft to see Goldie. 'Where's my champion racer?' he'll ask me. 'You said she was all right! You said she won the race!' Then what am I going to tell him?

'What's happened to Goldie?' I ask the other pigeons on the roof of the loft. But they're no help. They just fluff out their feathers and go, '*Cooooo*!'

Suddenly, I've got a sick feeling in my stomach. I've remembered what Grandad said last night. About the peregrine falcons in the old quarry. It makes me shudder.

'Goldie could outfly a dozen falcons,' I tell myself.

But a hawk can snatch a pigeon right out of the sky. Especially when it's tired at the end of the race. And when they eat one, there's nothing left but the feet.

I can see the old quarry from Grandad's garden. It's only across that field.

That's where those evil falcons have got their nest. I've just remembered what Grandad said last night: 'Someone should pull that nest down. Then they'll go away.'

I hate those falcons. They probably killed Goldie. I bet they did! I can feel myself getting really angry. My fists are all bunched up, in tight white knots.

I didn't know what to do before. I was all mixed up. But now I know exactly what to do. Now I know exactly what I can say to Grandad when he comes home.

I can say, 'I got rid of those falcons for you, Grandad. I did it, all on my own. They're never going to kill your racing pigeons again!'

4

In the quarry

It only takes five minutes to run to the old quarry.

My chest is burning when I get there and I'm gasping for breath but I don't stop. I go skidding down through the trees to the quarry floor.

I keep getting these awful pictures in my head. Of Goldie snatched out of the sky by cruel claws. Just as she's almost reached her home.

I can't bear to think about it. I've known Goldie ever since she was an egg. Ever since she was a tiny, helpless chick!

I want to get those falcons. I want revenge, for Goldie. I want to be able to tell Grandad, 'Take it easy, Grandad. You don't have to worry any more. I've taken care of those falcons for you!'

But I can't see any falcons. Where's their nest? I look around the quarry walls. That must be it. It's on the steepest side of the quarry. It looks like a big pile of sticks on a ledge. It's a long way up …

But then I think of Goldie, eaten, except for her feet.

I don't want to think any more. So I start climbing the quarry wall. Even though I can hardly see where I'm going. My eyes are all blurry with tears.

'I'll get you. I'll get you, falcons!' I shout up to the nest.

My voice doesn't sound like my voice. It sounds like a growling, angry bear.

It's not hard at all. I'm climbing fast – there are old tree roots to grab hold of. My hands are bleeding. But I don't feel the pain. I'm almost there.

Whoops! Some rocks go clattering down. My foot's slipped. I'm hanging on with my finger tips. I'm going to fall…!

Phew, found a foothold. Don't look down. I'm clinging like a starfish to the rock face. Only a little way to go. Don't look down.

My arms are so weak and trembly.
But I'm there.

'Got you!' I reach out my hand to
sweep the nest away. To send it
tumbling to the quarry floor.

Then I see the chick. I never
thought there'd be a chick! Its parents
aren't here to protect it. It's pink and
helpless, flopping about in the nest.

I think of Goldie, when she was small and helpless. When I looked after her.

I pull my hand back.

I can't do it. All my angry feelings gush away, like water down a plughole. I can't hurt that baby chick. Not even for Goldie. Not even for Grandad.

I start climbing again. Leaving the nest behind. I'm going up to the top of the quarry. There's not far to go. I'm almost there…

'*Oh no!*'

That's me, crying out. I just looked down. Big mistake! I feel sick. I feel dizzy. I can't move! I jam my hand into a gap in the rock so I don't fall.

What's that? It's a soft, feathery bundle.

'It's Goldie!'

She's squeezed herself into a tiny crack in the rock so the hawks can't see her.

I know straight away it's her. No other pigeon has got golden eyes like that. She's special. She's one in a million.

'It's all right,' I tell Goldie. 'I've found you now. You'll be all right now.'

I forget about being scared. I just grab Goldie, stuff her inside my shirt and haul myself up to the top of the quarry.

Safe!

For ages, I just lie in the grass, with my eyes closed. When the world stops spinning I open them.

The first thing I see is the falcons. They've come back. They're right above me, two of them, circling high in the sky. They go gliding down to their nest to feed their chick, their wings spread out like fans.

I just have to say, 'Wow!'

They're amazing. I can't seem to take my eyes off them. I never knew they were so beautiful.

Then I sit up and peek inside my shirt at Goldie. She looks very sick. She's a scrap of shivering feathers. And her golden eyes are dull. There's no sparkle in them.

'What's wrong, Goldie? Why didn't you fly home?'

Then I see what's wrong. It's her leg. It's tucked up underneath her. It looks like it's broken.

I stand up then and start running. My legs are still shaky from the climb. But I know I've got to get home quickly if I'm going to save Goldie's life.

5

Touch and go

It was touch and go with Goldie. I didn't think she would live. I've seen Grandad set pigeons' legs before. He does it with a cardboard tube and some sticky tape. But it's not as easy as it looks. When I tried it with Goldie my hands were shaking. I was so scared of hurting her.

But I did it. I took off her racing ring and taped up her broken leg. Then I put her in a shoebox in the pigeon loft.

She just sat there, looking miserable. I put some grains of corn in. She didn't eat them. I gave her some water. She didn't drink it. I thought, 'She'll be dead by morning.'

I couldn't sleep. I tossed and turned all night.

But, next morning, when I went round to the pigeon loft, she looked much better! She had a drink; she ate some corn. She even went 'Coo-coo' to me.

And in the weeks after that she grew stronger and stronger. Her golden eyes grew bright again.

Then, last night, Mum said to me, 'Grandad's coming home tomorrow.'

Well, I was really pleased. But I was really worried too. Because I haven't taken the splint off Goldie's leg yet. I don't know if it's mended properly. I don't know if she'll ever race again.

So here I am, sitting outside Grandad's pigeon loft, worried sick. He'll be coming home in about an hour's time.

I've got Goldie in my hands. I can feel her heart going *pit-a-pit-a-pat*. I've taken the splint off, just this minute. But I haven't let her fly yet. I daren't do it. But I have to. I have to find out if she can fly before Grandad gets here.

'Danny?'

Oh no! I know that voice. It's Grandad, coming down the garden. He's much sooner than I expected!

'There's my champion racer!' cries
Grandad.

He's got a stick to walk with. He sits
down beside me on the bench, slowly,
very slowly.

He strokes Goldie's feathers, gently,
with his finger.

Whoosh, whoosh. The other pigeons
whizz over our heads.

'Let her fly, Danny,' says Grandad.
'This is what I thought about every
day in hospital. Seeing my champion
racer fly.'

My stomach's doing back flips.
That's how nervous I am. But it's no
good putting it off any longer. I stand
up and hold Goldie high in the air.

'Come on, Goldie, come on, Goldie!' I whisper to her.

Then I toss her up into the sky.

She's flying! She flies straight and quick as an arrow to join the other birds. Sunshine's glittering on her wings.

'There goes my beauty!' cries Grandad.

I've still got some explaining to do. I'll have to tell Grandad the truth about Goldie. That she broke her leg. That she didn't win the race. But somehow I don't think he'll mind too much.

'Just look at her fly!' says Grandad. 'Look at my champion racer!'

In the distance, high over the old quarry, I can see three birds circling. Grandad can't see them because his eyes aren't so good. But I recognize them straight away. It's the young falcon, flying with its parents, riding the warm winds over the quarry.

'Come on, falcons!' I whisper. They're fantastic. They're brilliant fliers.

They'd better not catch my Goldie! That'd make me really sad. But I don't want to hurt them. I'm really glad I didn't do anything to hurt them that day I climbed the quarry wall. And if that sounds mixed-up I can't help it. That's the way I feel.

'What did you say just then about falcons?' asks Grandad. There's nothing wrong with his ears!

'Oh nothing,' I tell him. 'I'm just pleased you're back home, that's all.'

About the author

Once in County Durham where I live, I found a lost racing pigeon. It flew away before I could catch it. But I often wondered what happened to it and thought I might write a story about racing pigeons one day.

Then, later, I read a newspaper article. It was about pigeon fanciers who wanted to shoot birds of prey because they believed they were killing racing pigeons. This gave me lots of ideas. So finally, I sat down and wrote my racing pigeon story.

Other Treetops books at this level include:

I Wish, I Wish by Paul Shipton
The Personality Potion by Alan MacDonald
The Goalie's Secret by Paul Shipton
The Ultimate Trainers by Paul Shipton
The Case of the Smiling Shark by Tessa Krailing

Also available in packs

Stage 13 pack B	0 19 916918 7
Stage 13 class pack B	0 19 916919 5